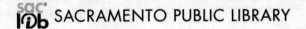

Carlos & Carmen

The Sandy Weekend

by Kirsten McDonald
illustrated by Erika Meza

Calico Kid

An Imprint of Magic Wagon
abdopublishing.com

For Pop and Daydee and all of our sandy weekends —**KKM**

This book is for José. Gracias por estar siempre ahí. —**EM**

abdopublishing.com

Published by Magic Wagon, a division of ABDO, PO Box 398166, Minneapolis, Minnesota 55439. Copyright © 2017 by Abdo Consulting Group, Inc. International copyrights reserved in all countries. No part of this book may be reproduced in any form without written permission from the publisher. Calico Kid™ is a trademark and logo of Magic Wagon.

Printed in the United States of America, North Mankato, Minnesota.
052016
092016

Written by Kirsten McDonald
Illustrated by Erika Meza
Edited by Heidi M.D. Elston
Designed by Candice Keimig

Library of Congress Cataloging-in-Publication Data

Names: McDonald, Kirsten, author. | Meza, Erika, illustrator.
Title: The sandy weekend / by Kirsten McDonald ; illustrated by Erika Meza.
Description: Minneapolis, MN : Magic Wagon, [2017] | Series: Carlos & Carmen
 | Summary: The Garcia family is spending a summer weekend at the beach, having a
 wonderful time playing in the water, and discovering the sand dollars and other small
 creatures that live along the shore.
Identifiers: LCCN 2015045665 | ISBN 9781624021428 (print) | ISBN 9781680779578 (ebook)
Subjects: LCSH: Hispanic American families--Juvenile fiction. | Twins--Juvenile fiction. | Brothers
 and sisters--Juvenile fiction. | Beaches--Juvenile fiction. | CYAC: Hispanic Americans--Fiction. |
 Twins--Fiction. | Brothers and sisters--Fiction. | Beaches--Fiction.
Classification: LCC PZ7.1.M4344 San 2016 | DDC 813.6--dc23
LC record available at http://lccn.loc.gov/2015045665

Table of Contents

Chapter 1
Happy Dancing

"Guess what!" Mamá said. "We're going on a trip today."

Carlos and Carmen were surprised.

"We're going to get salty and sandy," added Papá.

Carlos and Carmen were confused.

Tío Alex bounced his eyebrows. He said, "You're going to the beach."

Carlos and Carmen jumped out of their chairs with excited shouts.

Spooky jumped under the table. She liked excitement, but she liked being safe even more.

Carlos and Carmen happy-danced all around the table. Then the twins froze.

"Can Spooky come to the playa too?" they asked.

"A kitten at the playa?" cried Mamá. "No way!"

"I'll take care of Spooky," said Tío Alex.

Carlos and Carmen started happy-dancing again.

Carmen said, "We're going to build sand castles and jump in the olas."

"After jumping in the waves," said Carlos, "let's find seashells."

"Better than seashells," said Carmen, "let's find treasure!"

"Better than tesoro," said Carlos, "let's find pirate treasure!"

Tío Alex said, "If you find any tesoro, bring some back to me!"

Chapter 2
At the Beach

The Garcias drove and drove
and drove. At last, they were at
the beach.

"Let's jump in the agua," said Carlos. "Then let's dig with our palas."

Carmen said, "Race you to the olas."

Carlos chased Carmen to the water. Then they jumped through the waves.

"¡Mira!" said Carmen, and she did a handstand.

"Teach me!" Carlos shouted.

"Me too!" Papá shouted.

Carmen taught Carlos and Papá how to do handstands.

Mamá relaxed in the water nearby.

Suddenly the water around Mamá exploded with splashing.

Mamá stood up. She grinned an I'm-going-to-get-you grin. She splashed Carlos. She splashed Carmen. But mostly, she splashed Papá.

For the rest of the day, Carlos and Carmen jumped in the waves. They did handstands in the water. And, they dug for treasure.

Finally Mamá said, "It's time to go inside."

"Today was lots of fun," said Carlos. "But I still want to find some tesoro."

"Yo también," said Carmen with a yawn. "Tomorrow, we'll dig more holes with our palas. And mañana, we'll find some treasure."

Chapter 3
Treasure Time

The next day, Carlos and Carmen rode the waves. They watched tiny seashells burrow into the sand. And they built a really big sand castle.

They had sand in their hair. They had sand between their toes. They even had sand in their bathing suits.

"Let's explore the playa," suggested Mamá.

"Bring your buckets and palas," added Papá with a wink.

Carlos looked at Carmen. Carmen looked at Carlos. Then they shouted, "Treasure time!"

The Garcias set off down the beach. The twins looked for treasure, and they dug for treasure.

They found seashells and seaweed. They found crab shells and sea glass. But, they did not find any pirate treasure.

"Do you think we'll ever find any
treasure?" Carlos asked.

"Of course we will," Carmen told her
twin. "And the tesoro is going to be
big. It's going to be a million dollars."

"We can fill our buckets with the
treasure," added Carlos. "And we
can share it with Tío Alex. He'd like a
million dollars."

A little further down the beach,
the Garcias saw a sandbar out in the
water.

"There are polka dots all over that
sandbar," said Carlos.

"Let's go see what it is," said
Carmen.

The twins ran ahead. They splashed
through the water and onto the
sandbar.

There were sand dollars everywhere. Some were white, and some were grayish-greenish.

Carmen picked up a grayish-greenish sand dollar. Its tiny spikes wiggled and tickled her hand.

"It's alive," said Carmen.

"Wow!" said Carlos, picking up one. "How many do you think there are?"

"At least a hundred," said Carmen. "Maybe even a thousand."

"Or maybe a million," said Carlos. "A million sand dollars!"

"What did you just say?" asked Carmen.

"I said we found a million sand dollars," answered Carlos.

Carmen shouted, "Hooray! We found a million dollars! We found the treasure!"

Carlos and Carmen picked up one sand dollar after another. Soon their buckets were filled with the sandy treasure.

"¡Mira, Papá!" said Carmen, holding out her bucket. "We found the treasure!"

Carlos held his bucket out too. He said, "¡Mira, Mamá! We found a million dollars for Tío Alex!"

Mamá laughed and said, "Tío Alex is in for a big surprise mañana."

Chapter 4
Going Home

The next day, the Garcias waved good-bye to the beach.

Carlos said, "I want a playa at our house."

"Yo también," said Carmen.

Finally, they were home.

Carlos and Carmen jumped out of the car. They shouted, "Tío Alex! Spooky! We found the tesoro!"

"What!" said Tío Alex. "You found the treasure?"

Carmen said, "We found a million dollars!"

"A million dollars?" said Tío Alex.

The twins laughed and pounced on their uncle.

"You're teasing me," said Tío Alex. "There's no way you found a million dollars."

"Yes, we did," said Carlos and Carmen. "A million sand dollars!"

Everyone laughed and began to unload the car.

Carlos got his suitcase, and sand sprinkled onto the driveway.

Carmen got her suitcase, and sand spilled onto the driveway.

Each time something came out of the car, more sand fell onto the driveway.

Carlos looked at all of the sand. He smiled and said, "¡Mira! We got our wish. Now we have a playa at our house."

Then everyone went inside to tell Tío Alex and Spooky all about their sandy weekend.

Spanish
to
English

agua – water

Mamá – Mommy

mañana – tomorrow

¡Mira! – Look!

olas – waves

pala – shovel

Papá – Daddy

playa – beach

tesoro – treasure

Tío – Uncle

yo también – me too